Biscuit's Fun Treasury

four stories about everyone's favorite puppy

MY FIRST
I Can Read Book®

Biscuit's Fun Treasury

four stories about everyone's favorite puppy

by Alyssa Satin Capucilli

pictures by Pat Schories

CONTENTS

HarperCollins*Publishers*

MY FIRST
I Can Read Book®

Biscuit

story by ALYSSA SATIN CAPUCILLI
pictures by PAT SCHORIES

HarperTrophy®
A Division of HarperCollinsPublishers

Biscuit
Text copyright © 1996 by Alyssa Satin Capucilli
Illustrations copyright © 1996 by Pat Schories
Printed in the U.S.A. All rights reserved.

Library of Congress Cataloging-in-Publication Data
Capucilli, Alyssa Satin.
  Biscuit / story by Alyssa Satin Capucilli ; pictures by Pat Schories.
    p.   cm. — (My first I can read book)
Summary: A little yellow dog wants ever one more thing before he'll go to sleep.
  ISBN 0-06-026197-8. — ISBN 0-06-026198-6 (lib. bdg.)
  ISBN 0-06-444212-8 (pbk.)
  [1. Dogs—Fiction. 2. Bedtime—Fiction.] I. Schories, Pat, ill.
II. Title. III. Series.
PZ7.C179Bi   1997   95-9716
[E]—dc20   CIP
                                                                       AC

❖
First Harper Trophy edition, 1997

Visit us on the World Wide Web!
http://www.harperchildrens.com

For Laura and Peter who wait patiently
for a Biscuit of their very own
—A. S. C.

For Tess
—P. S.

This is Biscuit.

Biscuit is small.

Biscuit is yellow.

Time for bed, Biscuit!

Woof, woof!

Biscuit wants to play.

Time for bed, Biscuit!

Woof, woof!

Biscuit wants a snack.

Time for bed, Biscuit!

Woof, woof!

Biscuit wants a drink.

Time for bed, Biscuit!

Woof, woof!

Biscuit wants to hear a story.

Time for bed, Biscuit!

Woof, woof!

Biscuit wants his blanket.

Time for bed, Biscuit!

Woof, woof!

Biscuit wants his doll.

Time for bed, Biscuit!

Woof, woof!

Biscuit wants a hug.

Time for bed, Biscuit!

Woof, woof!

Biscuit wants a kiss.

Time for bed, Biscuit!

Woof, woof!

Biscuit wants a light on.

Woof!

Biscuit wants to be tucked in.

Woof!

Biscuit wants one more kiss.

Woof!

Biscuit wants one more hug.

Woof!

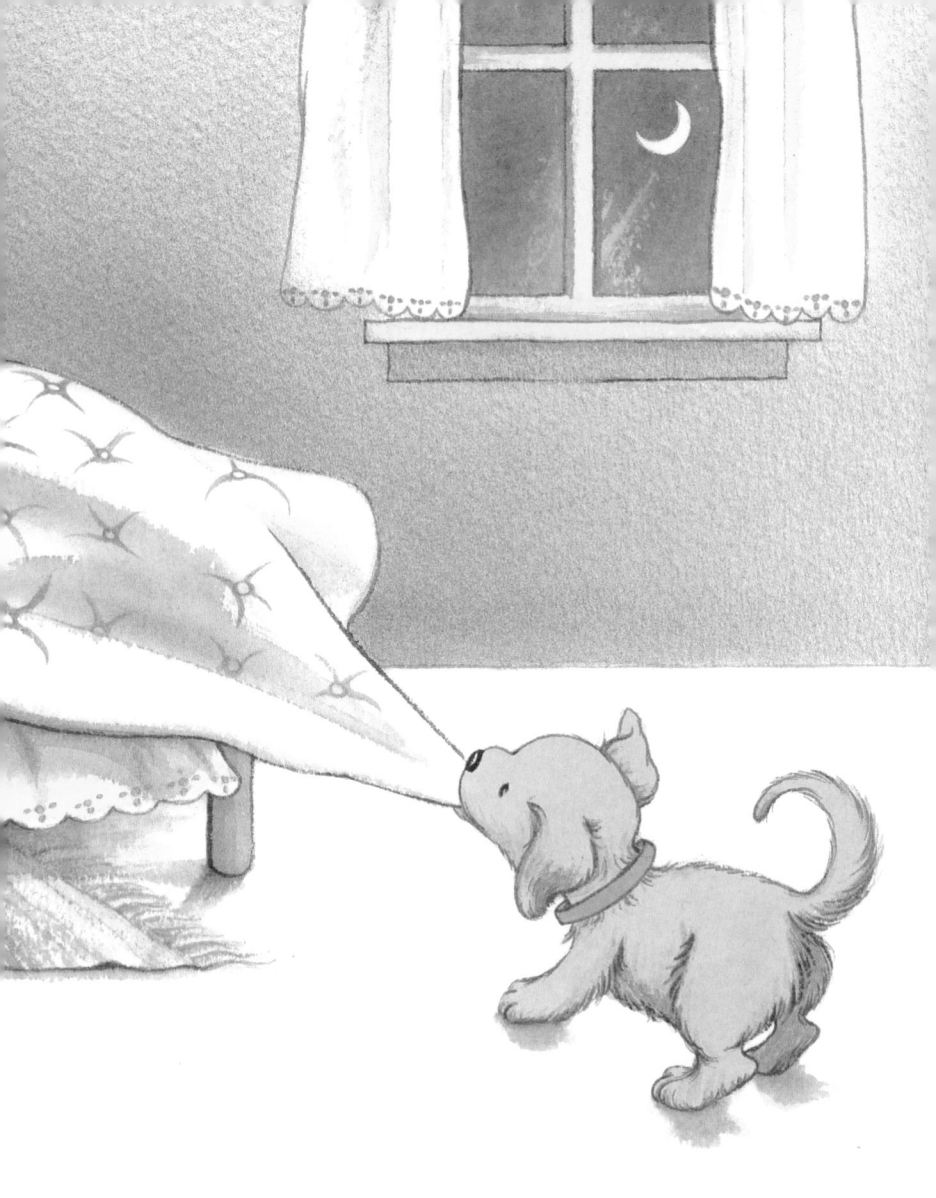

Biscuit wants to curl up.

Sleepy puppy.

Good night, Biscuit.

Biscuit
Finds a Friend

story by ALYSSA SATIN CAPUCILLI
pictures by PAT SCHORIES

HarperTrophy®
A Division of HarperCollinsPublishers

HarperCollins®, ☙®, Harper Trophy®, and I Can Read Book®
are trademarks of HarperCollins Publishers Inc.

Biscuit Finds a Friend
Text copyright © 1997 by Alyssa Satin Capucilli
Illustrations copyright © 1997 by Pat Schories
Printed in the U.S.A. All rights reserved.

Library of Congress Cataloging-in-Publication Data
Capucilli, Alyssa.
   Biscuit finds a friend / story by Alyssa Satin Capucilli ;
pictures by Pat Schories.
         p.   cm. — (A my first I can read book)
Summary: A puppy helps a little duck find its way home to the pond.
   ISBN 0-06-027412-3. — ISBN 0-06-027413-1 (lib. bdg.) —
   ISBN 0-06-444243-8 (pbk.)
   [1. Dogs—Fiction.   2. Ducks—Fiction.]   I. Schories, Pat, ill.   II. Title.
III. Series.
PZ7.C179Bis   1997   96-18368
[E]—dc20   CIP
                                                                        AC

First Harper Trophy edition, 1998
❖
Visit us on the World Wide Web!
http://www.harperchildrens.com

For two very special friends,
Margaret Jean O'Connor and Willie Hornick.

Woof! Woof!

What has Biscuit found?

Is it a ball?

Woof!

Is it a bone?

Woof!

Quack!

It is a little duck.

The little duck is lost.

Woof! Woof!

We will bring
the little duck
back to the pond.

Woof! Woof!

Here, little duck.

Here is the pond.

Here are your mother
and your father.
Quack!

Here are your brothers
and your sisters.
Quack! Quack!

The ducks say thank you.
Thank you for finding
the little duck.

Quack!
The little duck
wants to play.

Quack!
Woof!

Quack!
Woof!

Splash!

Biscuit fell into the pond!

Silly Biscuit.

You are all wet!

Woof!

Oh no, Biscuit.

Not a big shake!

Woof!

Time to go home, Biscuit.

Quack! Quack!

Say good-bye, Biscuit.

Woof! Woof!

Good-bye, little duck.

Biscuit has found
a new friend.

My First
I Can Read Book®

Bathtime for Biscuit

by ALYSSA SATIN CAPUCILLI
pictures by PAT SCHORIES

HarperTrophy®
A Division of HarperCollinsPublishers

Bathtime for Biscuit
Text copyright © 1998 by Alyssa Satin Capucilli
Illustrations copyright © 1998 by Pat Schories
Printed in the U.S.A. All rights reserved.

Library of Congress Cataloging-in-Publication Data
Capucilli, Alyssa.
  Bathtime for Biscuit / story by Alyssa Satin Capucilli ; pictures by
Pat Schories.
      p.   cm. —(A my first I can read book)
  Summary: Biscuit the puppy runs away from his bath with his puppy friend Puddles.
  ISBN 0-06-027937-0. — ISBN 0-06-027938-9 (lib. bdg.)
  ISBN 0-06-444264-0 (pbk.)
  [1. Dogs—Fiction.   2. Baths—Fiction.]   I. Schories, Pat, ill.   II. Title.   III. Series.
PZ7.C179Bat   1998   97-49663
[E]—dc21   CIP
                                                                                            AC

First Harper Trophy edition, 1999
❖
Visit us on the World Wide Web!
http://www.harperchildrens.com

This one is for my parents.
—A.S.C.

To Sri K.
—P.S.

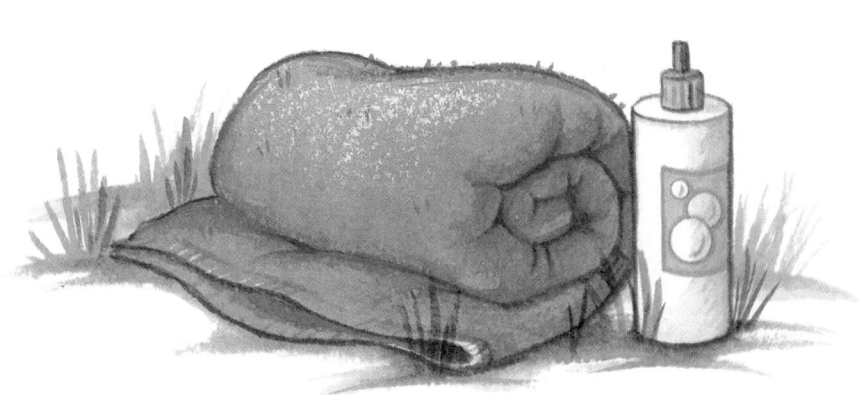

Time for a bath, Biscuit!

Woof, woof!

Biscuit wants to play.

Time for a bath, Biscuit!

Woof, woof!

Biscuit wants to dig.

Time for a bath, Biscuit!

Woof, woof!

Biscuit wants to roll.

Time for a bath, Biscuit!

Time to get nice and clean.

Woof, woof!

In you go!

Woof!

Biscuit does not want a bath!

Bow wow!
Biscuit sees
his friend Puddles.

Woof, woof!

Biscuit wants to climb out.

Come back, Biscuit!

Woof!

Come back, Puddles!

Bow wow!

Biscuit and Puddles
want to play
in the sprinkler.

Biscuit and Puddles
want to dig
in the mud.

Biscuit and Puddles
want to roll
in the flower bed.

Now I have you!

Woof, woof!

Let go of the towel,

Biscuit!

Bow wow!

Let go of the towel,

Puddles!

Silly puppies!

Let go!

Woof, woof!

Bow wow!

Oh!

Time for a bath, Biscuit!

Woof, woof!

A bath for all of us!

28

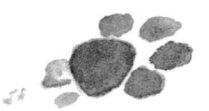

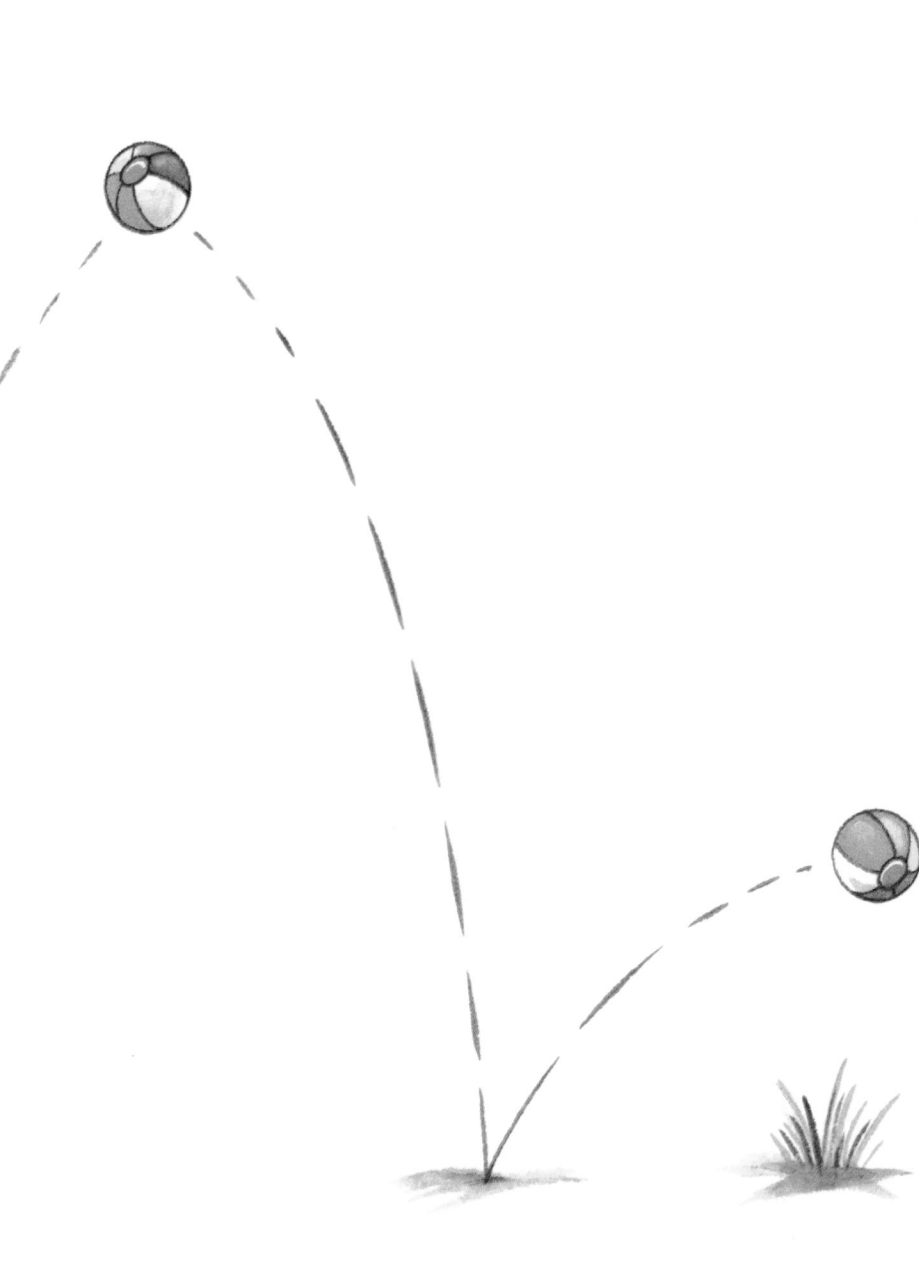

MY FIRST
I Can Read Book®

Biscuit's New Trick

story by ALYSSA SATIN CAPUCILLI
pictures by PAT SCHORIES

HarperTrophy®
An Imprint of HarperCollinsPublishers

Biscuit's New Trick
Text copyright © 2000 by Alyssa Satin Capucilli
Illustrations copyright © 2000 by Pat Schories
Printed in the U.S.A. All rights reserved.

Library of Congress Cataloging-in-Publication Data
Capucilli, Alyssa.
   Biscuit's new trick / story by Alyssa Satin Capucilli ; pictures by Pat Schories.
      p.   cm. — (My first I can read book)
   Summary: A puppy does all sorts of tricks in the process of learning the one his
master is trying to teach him.
   ISBN 0-06-028067-0. — ISBN 0-06-028068-9 (lib. bdg.)
   ISBN 0-06-444308-6 (pbk.)
   [1. Dogs—Training—Fiction.]   I. Schories, Pat, ill.   II. Title.   III. Series.
PZ7.C179Biu   2000   99-23004
[E]—dc21   CIP

First Harper Trophy edition, 2001
❖
Visit us on the World Wide Web!
www.harperchildrens.com

For Anthony and Ruby, the newest
—A.S.C.

To Laura
—P.S.

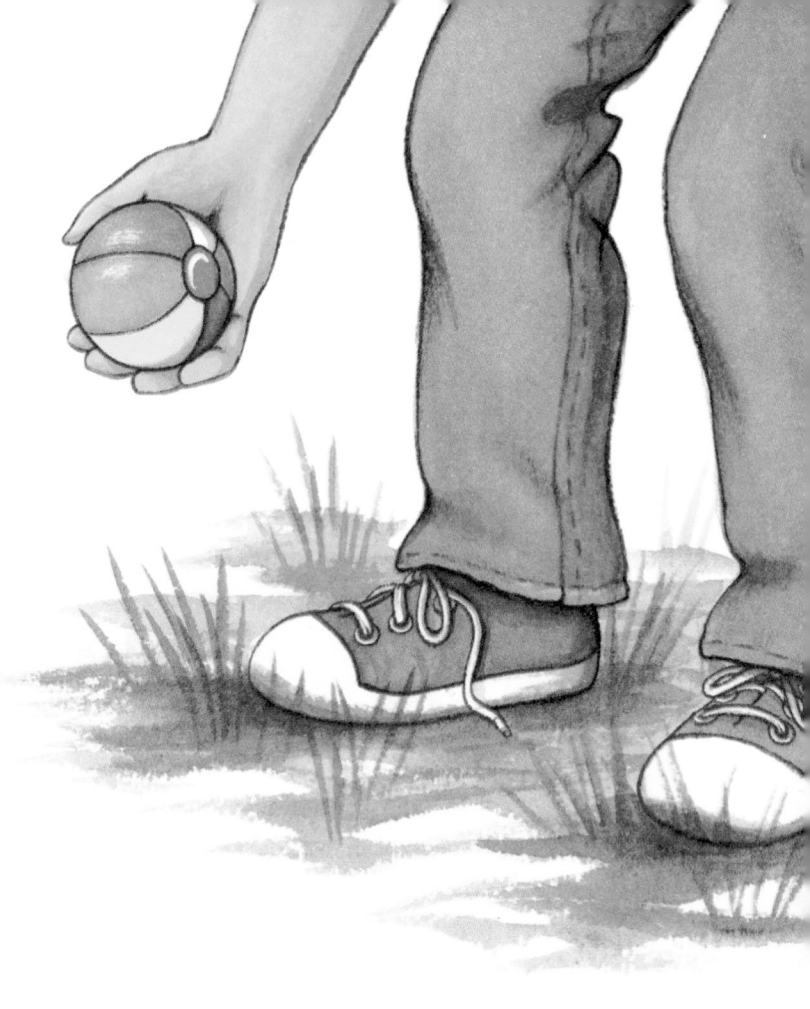

Here, Biscuit!

Look what I have.

Woof, woof!

It's time to learn
a new trick, Biscuit.
Woof, woof!

It's time to learn
to fetch the ball.
Ready?

Fetch the ball, Biscuit.

Woof, woof!

Silly puppy!

Don't roll over now.

Get the ball, Biscuit.

Fetch the ball, Biscuit.

Woof, woof!

Where are you going,
Biscuit?
Woof!

Funny puppy!
Fetch the ball,
not your bone.

12

Let's try again.

Fetch the ball, Biscuit!

Woof, woof!

Good puppy!
You got the ball.
Woof!

Wait, Biscuit.

16

Bring the ball back!
Woof, woof!

Let's try one more time.

Fetch the ball, Biscuit!

Woof, woof!

Oh no!

Not in the mud!

Stop, Biscuit!
Don't fetch it now!
Woof!

Oh, Biscuit!

You did it!

You learned a new trick!

Woof, woof!

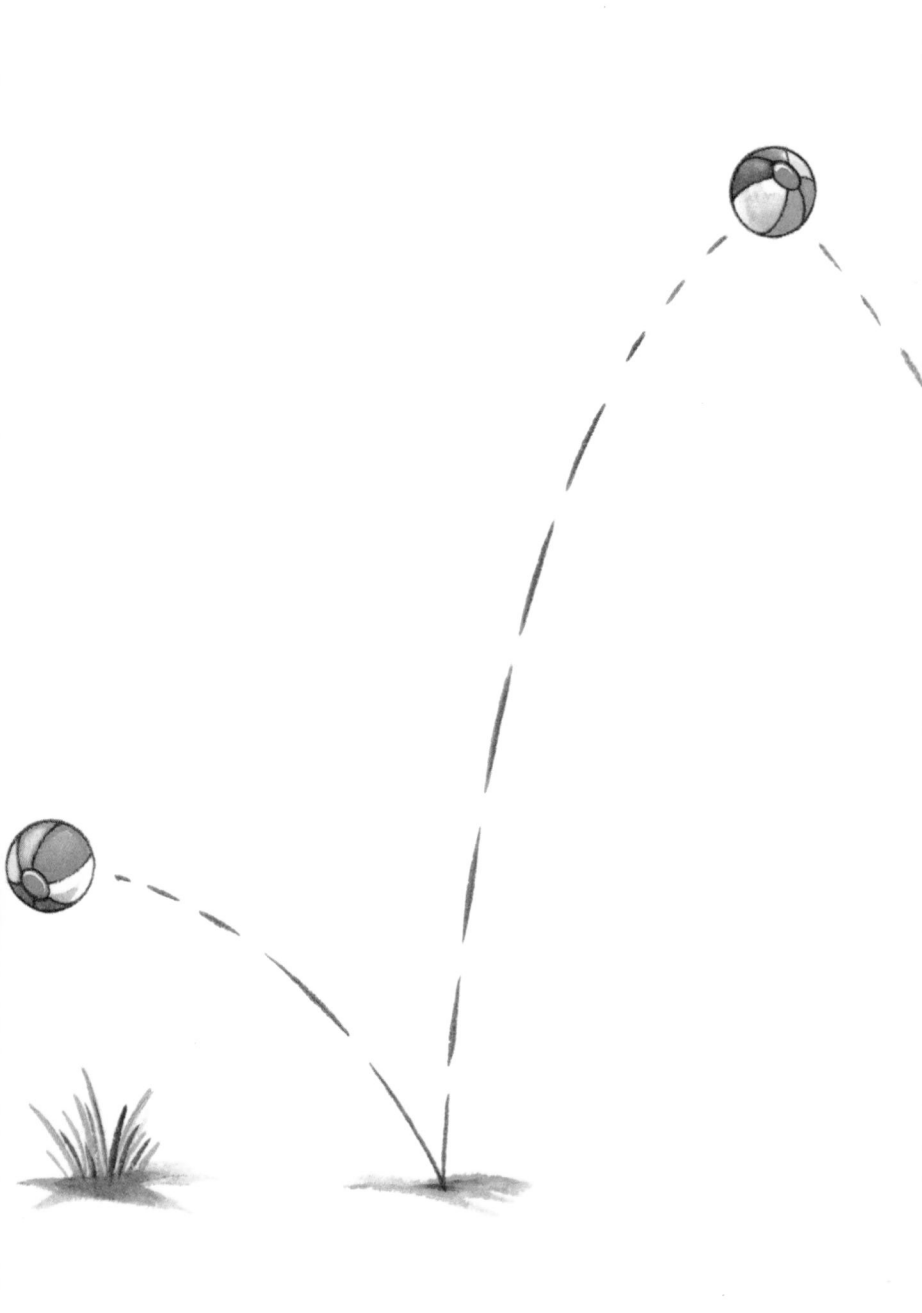

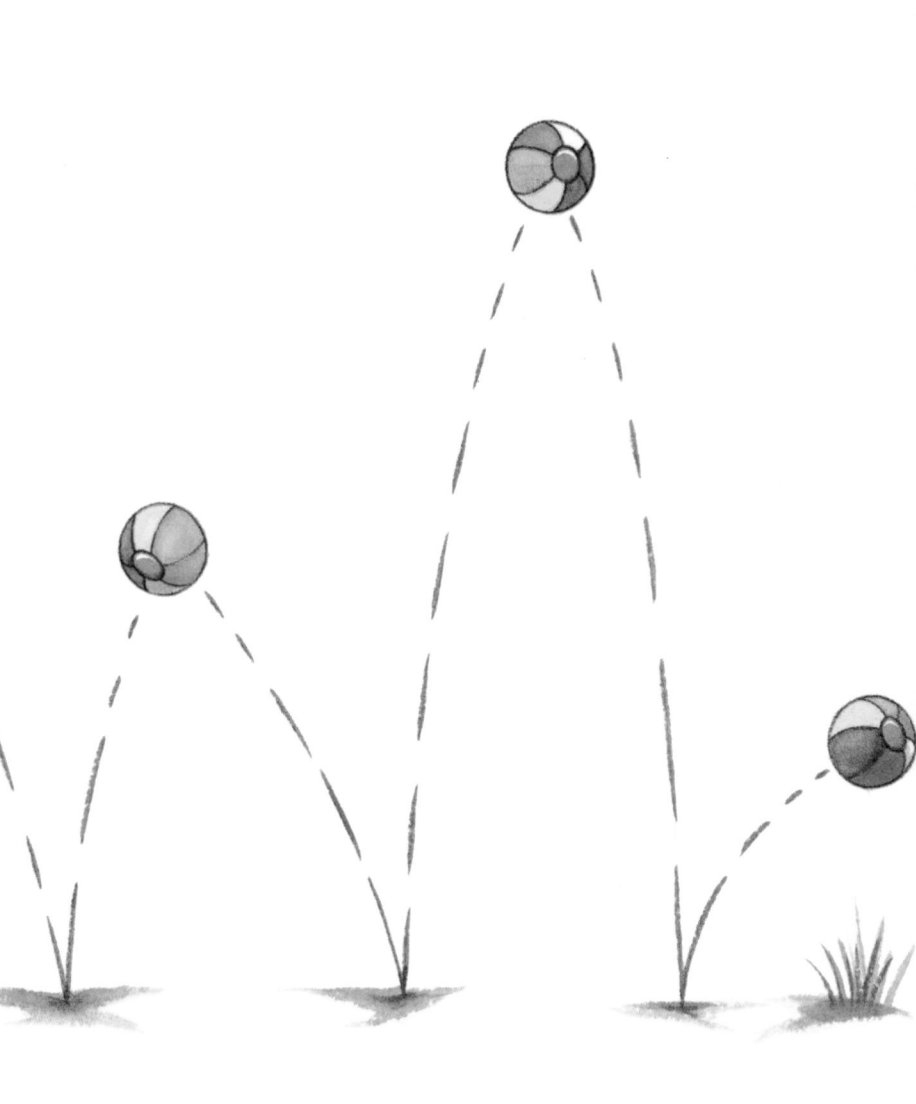